KOMODO!

by Peter Sis

Greenwillow Books, New York

Pen and ink and watercolor paints were used for the full-color art.
The text type is Adroit Medium.

Printed in Singapore by Tien Wah Press
First Edition   10 9 8 7 6 5 4 3 2 1

Library of Congress Cataloging-in-Publication Data
Sis, Peter.
Komodo! / by Peter Sis.
p.   cm.
Summary: A young boy who loves dragons goes
with his parents to the Indonesian island of
Komodo in hopes of seeing a real dragon.
Includes factual information about the Komodo dragon.
ISBN 0-688-11583-7 (trade).
ISBN 0-688-11584-5 (lib. bdg.)
1. Komodo dragon—Juvenile fiction.
[1. Komodo dragon—Fiction.
2. Lizards—Fiction.]   I. Title.
PZ7.S6219Ko   1993   [E]—dc20
92-25811   CIP   AC

**To the Lajtha family
of intrepid travelers**

It is always easy to find me in school pictures because of my dragon T-shirt.

I have loved
dragons as
long as
I can
remember.

That's why my parents decided to take me to Indonesia. There are real dragons on the island of Komodo.

KOMODO DRAGON
(VARANUS KOMODOENSIS)

THE KOMODO DRAGON IS A MONITOR LIZARD WITH SHARP CLAWS AND FEARSOME-LOOKING JAWS. ITS BODY CAN BE UP TO 9 FEET LONG, AND IT CAN WEIGH OVER 300 POUNDS. ITS LONG TONGUE, FORKED LIKE A SNAKE'S, IS BOTH AN ORGAN OF SMELL AND OF TASTE. DRAGONS CAN LOCATE CARRION BY SMELL OVER 5 MILES AWAY. THEY HAVE BEEN KNOWN TO COME INTO A VILLAGE IN BROAD DAYLIGHT TO STEAL GOATS. NATIVES CALL THE GIANT REPTILE ORA. SOME PEOPLE BELIEVE THE CHINESE DRAGON WAS MODELED AFTER THE KOMODO DRAGON. IT IS EXTINCT EVERYWHERE IN THE WORLD EXCEPT ON KOMODO AND NEIGHBORING ISLANDS. PEOPLE HAVE BEEN KNOWN TO DISAPPEAR ON KOMODO.

KOMODO

I re-read my book on Komodo dragons on the plane.

KOMODO DRAGON LIVES ON THE ISLAND OF KOMODO IN INDONESIA
(SOUTHEAST ASIA)

A KOMODO DRAGON CAN GO UP TO $1\frac{1}{2}$ MONTHS WITHOUT WATER. LARGE DRAGONS CAN KILL WATER BUFFALO 15 TIMES THEIR WEIGHT. THEY OFTEN STRIKE THEIR PREY WITH THEIR TAILS. UNLIKE OTHER REPTILES, THEIR BODY TEMPERATURE REMAINS UNIFORM DAY AND NIGHT. THE LIFE SPAN OF A DRAGON IS ABOUT 50 YEARS. IN FEBRUARY THEY SHED THEIR SKIN.

RUNS SWIFTLY

SWIMS

DIVES

DIGS

WALKS ON TWO FEET

CLIMBS

I imagined
exactly how
it would be.

We landed
in Bali
and did
some
sightseeing.

The next day
we got on
a ship to
Komodo.

It wasn't
at all
the way
I expected
it to be.

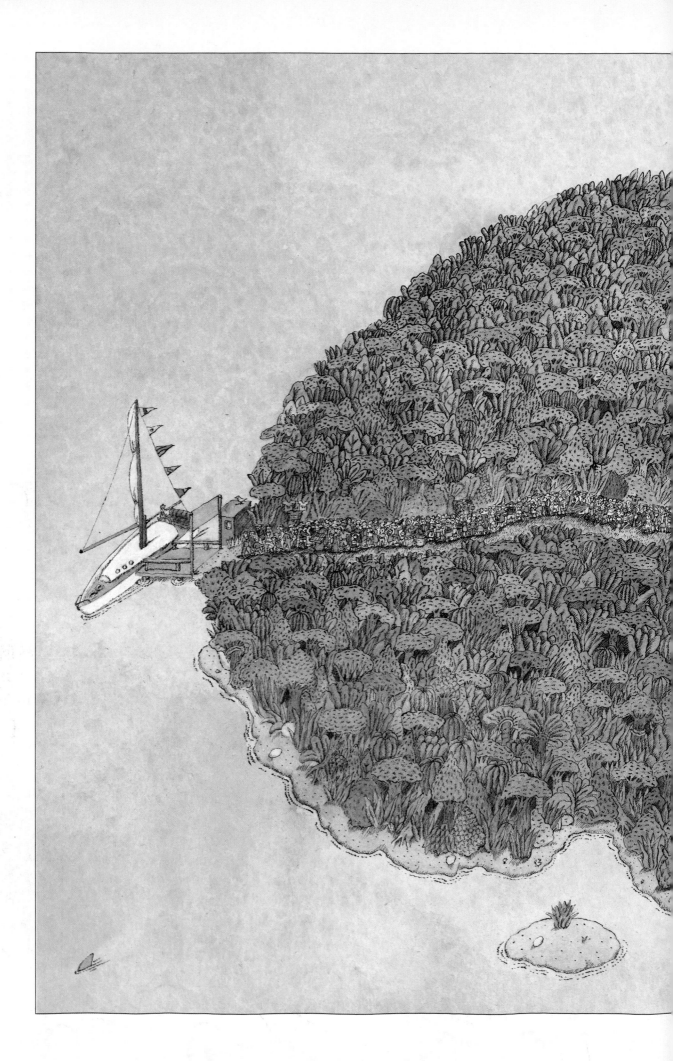

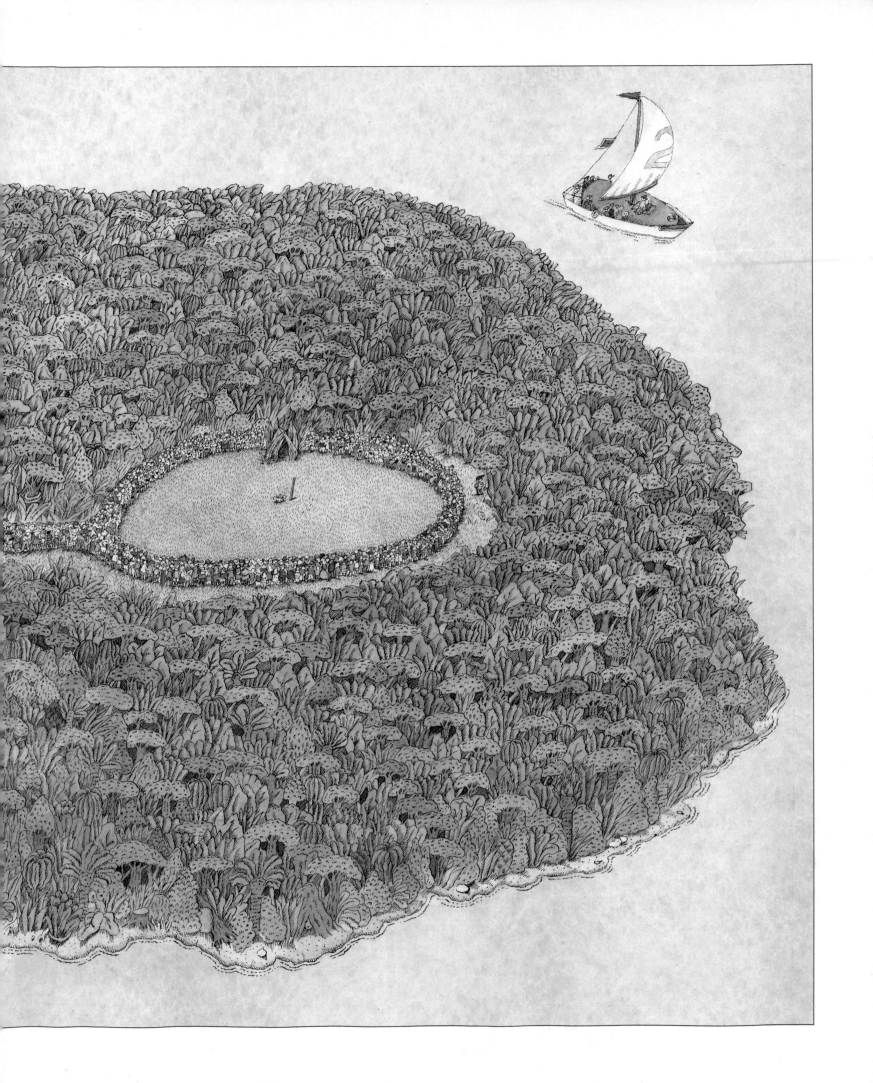

There were so many people waiting for the Dragon Show that I couldn't see anything.

I told
my parents
I'd be
right back.

Suddenly
I heard
a roar.

A dragon!

Then
it was gone.
Or was it?

My parents
were
disappointed
with Komodo,
but I thought
it was the
best place
I'd ever been.

The island of Komodo in Indonesia is the world's largest undisturbed habitat of the Komodo dragon. This giant monitor lizard—the biggest on earth, with an individual life span of fifty to sixty years—is the sole survivor of the carnivorous dinosaurs that thrived in tropical Asia 130 million years ago. It is considered to be the last of its kind inhabiting the world today.

This creature (*Varanus komodoensis*), called *ora* (land crocodile) by the natives, was thought to be only a myth until the turn of the century when it was sighted by pearl fishermen who had been forced to land on Komodo during a storm.

Komodo dragons also live in some other parts of Indonesia, but only a few specimens of this rare species can be found in the world's zoos.